Wow!

It's great being a duck

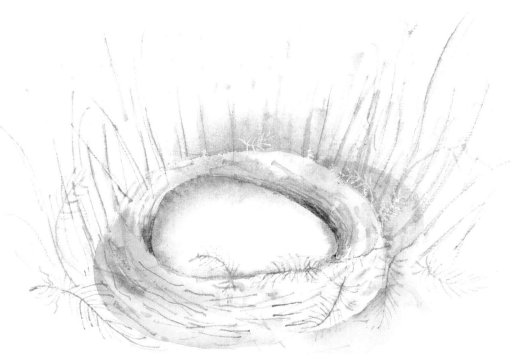

1 3 5 7 9 10 8 6 4 2

Copyright © Joan Rankin 1997

Joan Rankin has asserted her right under the Copyright, Designs and Patents Act, 1988
to be identified as the author and illustrator of this work.

First published in the United Kingdom in 1997 by The Bodley Head Children's Books,
Random House, 20 Vauxhall Bridge Road, London, SW1V 2SA

Random House Australia (Pty) Limited, 20 Alfred Street, Milsons Point, Sydney,
New South Wales 2061, Australia

Random House New Zealand Limited, 18 Poland Road, Glenfield,
Auckland 10, New Zealand

Random House South Africa (Pty) Limited, Endulini, 5A Jubilee Road,
Parktown 2193, South Africa

Random House UK Limited Reg. No. 954009

A CIP catalogue record for this book is available from the British Library

ISBN 0 370 32364 5

Printed in Hong Kong

Wow!
It's great being a duck

Story and pictures by
Joan Rankin

THE BODLEY HEAD
London

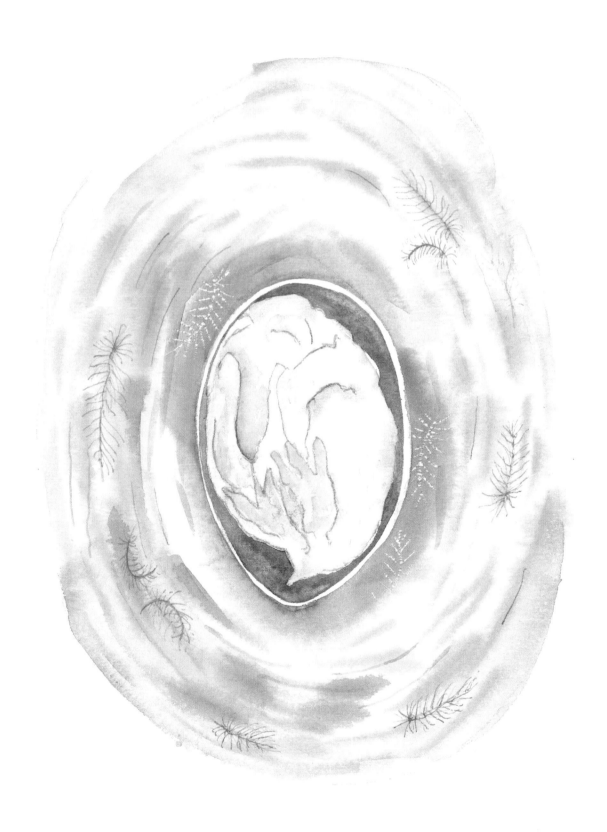

Lillee was the last born,
the last to hatch, and the smallest and skinniest.

All the other ducklings
had already left the nest when, at last,
Lillee's egg began to crack. Lillee peeped out...

She saw her mother's *eye*,

then she saw her mother's *feathers*

and her mother's *feet.*

CRASH!

Lillee fell out of her egg
into the BIG WORLD.

Lillee's mother was very proud.
She wanted **everyone**
to admire tiny Lillee.

"Come swim! Come swim!"
quacked her older brothers and sisters.

"Come along, Lillee," coaxed Mother Duck.
"You must learn to swim or
Furry-legs, Long-tail, Sharp-snout, Pink-tongue Fox
will gobble you up."

But Lillee did not want to take her feet off the ground.

So while her brothers and sisters
were swimming and diving,

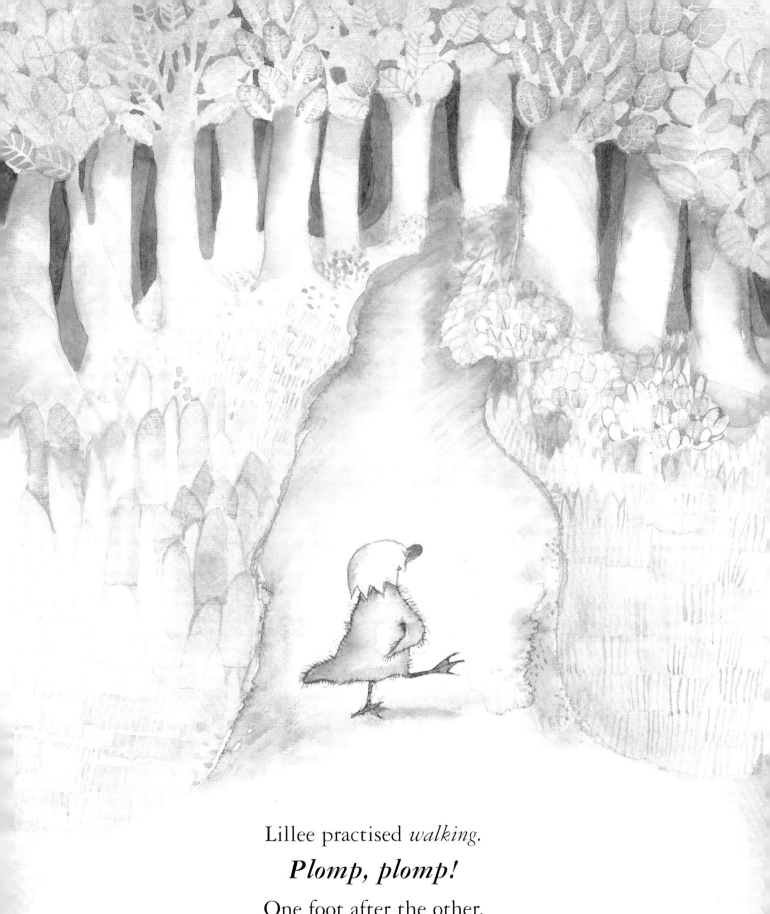

Lillee practised *walking*.

Plomp, plomp!

One foot after the other,

into the dark, green forest she *walked*.

Along the long and winding path she went until she met Mr Furry-legs.

"What's a nice little duck like you doing in the dark, green forest?" asked Mr Furry-legs.

"I'm walking," replied Lillee proudly.

"You are very small and skinny," remarked Mr Furry-legs.
"I will show you where you can eat tender nasturtium leaves.
You need **fattening up!**"

Lillee ate so many nasturtium leaves,
she could hardly waddle home.

A week later she met Mr Furry-legs-Long-tail.

"My, you do walk well... for a duck,"

said Mr Furry-legs-Long-tail.

"Thank you," said Lillee.

"I shall never take my feet off the ground.

It's far too dangerous."

"I love walking, too," said Mr Furry-legs-Long-tail. "Let's stroll together into the forest. And I'll show you some tasty things for a growing duck like you to eat."

Lillee ate many wild berries.

She ate until her beak turned purple.

She ate until her feathers turned purple.

"How do you feel?" asked her new friend.

"Fat!" replied Lillee.

"Good," said Mr Furry-legs-Long-tail.

"I like fat ducks."

The following week Lillee returned to the berry patch.

And there she met Mr Furry-legs-Long-tail-Sharp-snout.

While she looked for any remaining berries they spoke.

"Do you have a large family?" asked her companion.

"Oh, yes," said Lillee, "I have lots of big brothers and sisters."

"Really? Then I must show you where to find snails.

I believe they are very good for making ducks

BIG...strong...*and* **fat.**"

The snails were so tasty, so absolutely scrumptious,
Lillee stayed until she had eaten every one.
"Do bring your brothers and sisters next time,"
called Mr Furry-legs-Long-tail-Sharp-snout.
"Okay!" said Lillee.
"But they can't walk as quickly as I can."
And off she waddled,
her tail dragging on the ground.

The next week Mr Furry-legs-Long-tail-Sharp-snout-Pink-tongue
came walking along the forest path.
There he found Lillee sitting alone
on the path, sobbing.
"Why are you crying all by
yourself?" he asked.
"My family have flown away to a
bigger pond," she wailed.
"Oh dear, I was hoping to have a party
with all of you. But why don't you come along with me?"

Lillee stopped crying.
"You are kind," she sniffed as she got up to follow her
new friend into the dark, green forest.

"Hurry! Hurry! You really must walk a little faster,"
said Mr Furry-legs-Long-tail-Sharp-snout-Pink-tongue, licking his lips.
How rude! thought Lillee, resting for a while.
"Come on! Come on!" he snarled at her.
"Just who does he think he is?" quacked Lillee, looking up.

She *glared* at his furry legs.

She studied his LONG TAIL.

She observed his sharp snout.
She ogled as his pink tongue
slipped across a row of needle-sharp teeth.

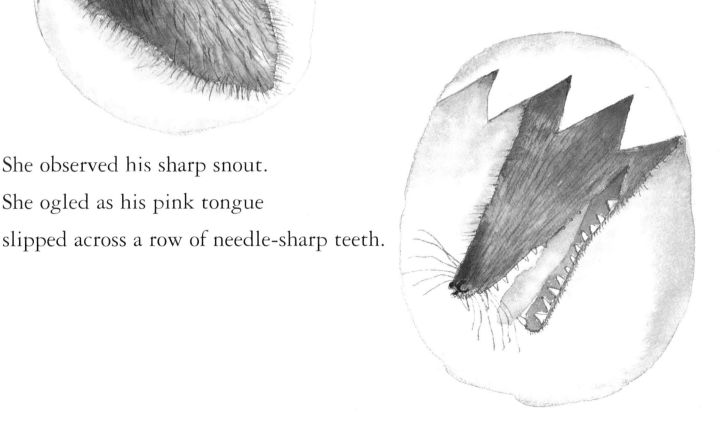

Lillee *squeaked* and Lillee *squawked when she saw....*

Mr Furry-legs,

Long-tail,

Sharp-snout,

Pink-tongue,

FOX!

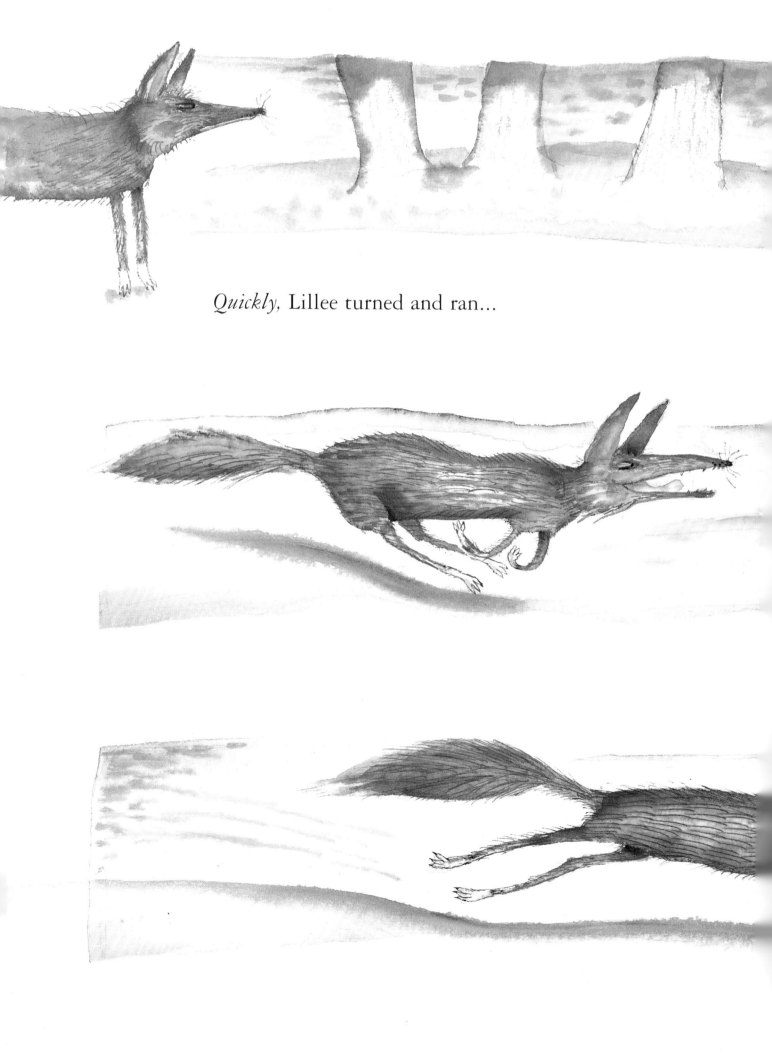

Quickly, Lillee turned and ran...

flap, flap, **flop, flop!**

Faster and faster along the winding path

through the dark, green forest

back to the pond.

SPLASH! into the pond.
Paddle, paddle, *faster and faster.*

Lillee could hear the panting breath of Mr Fox.
She could feel his prickly whiskers on her tail.

Paddle, paddle went her feet.
Flap, flap went her wings.

suddenly...

Lillee was flying!

Up, up, over the pond.   Up, up, over the trees.

Right out of the reach of Mr Fox.

Up, up over the hills and onto the other side.

Below in a big pond she saw her family.

Down she glided and landed just like an expert.

"Look, look!" quacked her brothers and sisters.

"Hey, Lillee! We thought you could only walk!"

"So did I," said Lillee. "But now I can do everything!"

And she could!